LIBRARIES NI
WITHDRAWN FROM STOCK

D1102348

FAIRY TALES GONE BAD

ZOMBIERELLA

By

Joseph Coelho

Illustrated by

Freya Hartas

WALKER
BOOKS

This is a work of fiction. Names, characters, places and incidents
are either the product of the author's imagination or, if real, used
fictitiously. All statements, activities, stunts, descriptions, information
and material of any other kind contained herein are included for
entertainment purposes only and should not be relied on for
accuracy or replicated as they may result in injury.

First published in Great Britain 2020 by Walker Books Ltd
87 Vauxhall Walk, London SE11 5HJ

2 4 6 8 10 9 7 5 3 1

Text © 2020 Joseph Coelho
Illustrations © 2020 Freya Hartas

The right of Joseph Coelho and Freya Hartas to be identified as author and
illustrator of this work has been asserted by them in accordance with the
Copyright, Designs and Patents Act 1988

This book has been typeset in Archer

Printed and bound in Italy

All rights reserved. No part of this book may be reproduced, transmitted or
stored in an information retrieval system in any form or by any means, graphic,
electronic or mechanical, including photocopying, taping and recording, without
prior written permission from the publisher.

British Library Cataloguing in Publication Data:
a catalogue record for this book is available from the British Library

ISBN 978-1-4063-8966-1

www.walker.co.uk

MIX
Paper from
responsible sources
FSC® C023419

*For all the children I had the pleasure
of working with over the years who were
hungry for some gruesome tales. – J.C.*

*For Sam the zombie boyfriend and Katsu
the vampire cat. – F.H.*

CONTENTS

The Librarian

Hello, I'm The Librarian.
I used to believe in nice things!
Sweet things.
Fairy tales and butterflies
that don't bite.
Then I began to work in the library.
In the reference section.
The section for adults only
where there are big books,
dangerous books,
forbidden books.

I spent my days stamping books,
shelving books
and reading ... books.
I found a hidden section at the back of the library,
covered in powdery dust as thick as snow.
A section full of old books,
unread books,
unthumbed books,
unloved books.

You know how when you leave fruit in a bowl
uneaten, it goes off?
Mould starts to bloom on the skin,
the flesh goes brown and soft,
flies lay eggs, maggots squirm,
horrid smells find their way into the fruit...
The same happens with books!

The same had happened to these books.
These books, these fairy tales, had gone off.

Their covers were swollen, cracked leather.
Their spines were bent and creased.
Their covers strained against the chains
that bound them.
A padlock, orange with rust,
decorated with the gaping, snarling face of
a demon,
its terrifying mouth forming the keyhole,
kept the books locked tight.
I had the key,
this key.

I slipped it into the mouth of the demon padlock.
It chewed at the key.
The key was hard to turn,
creaking and groaning,
metal against metal.

I twisted with all my might until
the lock sprang open.
I wrestled the chains off the books and
peered at their titles, and this is what I found...

Goldilocks and the Three Bears
had changed its title to ...
Grannylocks.

The Ugly Duckling had changed its title to ...
The Monstrous Duckling.

Jack and the Beanstalk had become ...
Jack and the Flesh-Eating Beanstalk.

The Boy Who Cried Wolf had become ...
The Boy Who Puked Up a Wolf.

Sleeping Beauty had become ...
Creeping Beauty.

And *Cinderella* had become ...

ZOMBIERELLA!!!

I took *Zombierella* off the shelf.

Its pages were musty smelling.

This book had not been read for a

very long time –

it was very off!

Way past its sell-by date!

Inside I found all sorts of horrible,

disgusting, foul and nasty changes to the story...

I started to read and, as I read, I began

to change.

I was no longer just a librarian of normal books,

I was The Librarian of decrepit stories,

ragged legends,

putrid parables.

I was The Librarian of fairy tales

that had gone ...

BAD!!!

The Digging of a Grave

It was on the dullest days
with the greyest skies
that Cinderella missed her father most.

He was buried out back.
Under a flint grey tombstone
in Lumpkin's field,
where the nettles and brambles
made way for the poppies.

She'd visit his grave
whenever she could.
Her faithful horse Lumpkin
nuzzling at her side.
Her one friend.
Her only family.

She rode Lumpkin over the grey fields,
the last scraps
of her father's lands,
in a dress of rags and hand-me-downs
to feel free.

Clutching onto Lumpkin's greying mane
they rode the stubble
of their neglected crops.
Lumpkin didn't go
as fast as he used to.
His gallop was more
pained trot

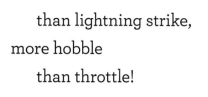

than lightning strike,
more hobble
    than throttle!

The bones
of his once muscular back
stuck painfully into Cinderella,
but she needed to ride him
        one
                last
                        time.
From the field's edge
she could see the winding,
dusty road that ran into
Grimmsville.
A town with glamour
long behind it,
it now sat festering ...
                forgotten.

As she stroked Lumpkin's grey coat,
she noticed how his breath
came in long, wizened puffs,
how his rib cage rattled,
how his once strong legs shook.

"It's OK, Lumpkin, we'll rest now."

Lumpkin whinnied in appreciation.
Though if he could,
he'd run to the silver moon for her.
They started to turn back when
Cinderella's gaze
was hooked,
    shooked,
        drawn in by
the old abandoned mansion
    at the top
        of the hill.

A mansion with five towers
spread like fingers
rising up out of a palm.
Both terrible
and beautiful.
    Both fist and grab.

>   *Dum dum!*
>   *Dum dum!*
>   *Dum dum!*

The horses
were larger than any
Cinderella had ever seen.
Blacker than the backs of eyelids
during nightmares.
They were galloping up the winding road
that led to the mansion
up on the hill.

There were three
groups of six

horses each pulling
a carriage unlike

anything Cinderella had
ever, ever seen.

The carriages
were low
    so
        low.

Reminding her of something
she couldn't quite remember.
And coloured a deep black
that refused to reflect
the setting sun.

From behind the last carriage
a wisp,
    a cloud
        was rising,

heading towards Cinderella and Lumpkin
like a dark omen.
Lumpkin attempted a whinny
but it came out like a rasp.

"It's OK, Lumpy."

The cloud got closer
        like a swarm
            of bats.
Cinderella could feel her heart
start
to rush.
Lumpkin's muscles began
a slow twitch
beneath her.

"Please, Lumpy, one more time, just for me.
Let's show them the meaning of speed."

Cinderella dug her heels
into Lumpkin's bony side
and immediately felt a pang of regret.
But it stirred in him
a memory,
a shadow
of his former self.
And for the briefest of moments,
he felt the pulse of youth
thrum in his veins.
They were off at a gallop,
the cloud of bats
falling behind.

"Wahoooooooo!"

exalted Cinderella.

But as soon as the shout left her lips,
Lumpkin began to slow
    and shake
        and stumble
            and stall.

And the bats clustered closer,
only they weren't bats.
Cinderella now could see that they
looked more like...

*"Paper ... they are black sheets of paper,
Lumpy,
of the weightiest, most luxuriating
stationery!"*

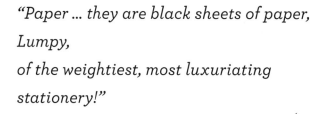

The black sheets of paper
were scattering into the wind.
Most were heading towards the town,
but one lone sheet was
swooping down onto Cinderella.
It slipped itself
into her hand ...

it was a flyer
on cave black paper that stained Cinderella's
fingers.
And printed upon it,
in the thickest and reddest ink...

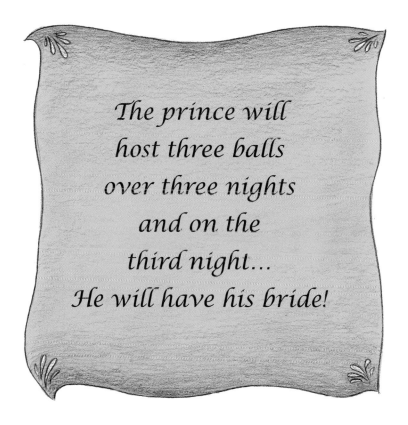

*The prince will
host three balls
over three nights
and on the
third night...
He will have his bride!*

"Looks like a prince is moving into
the old abandoned mansion, Lumpkin,"
said Cinderella, as they plodded
back to her father's grave,
knowing full well that
an invitation to a ball,
    any ball,
        would never,
            could never,
                be for her.

Lumpkin's eyes were two watery pools
as he kneeled by Cinderella,
his rattling breath
echoing through his skeletal frame.

An apple tree grew bent and heavy
above her father's grave.
Cinderella picked an apple
redder than the setting sun

and fed it to her faithful friend.

In her heart she knew
that her beloved Lumpkin
would soon be gone
and she would be left alone
with them,
her so-called family,
in the house,
the house that was hers,
that should have been hers,
but now was theirs.

A house that once
glittered with joy
but now
was sunk in darkness.

Lumpkin's head rested
on Cinderella's lap,

37

each breath taking longer
than the last.
The sun dipped lower,
redder in the sky.

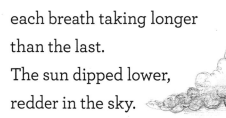

She knew this day would come,
knew her friend was old,
knew he would have to leave.
But the knowing
made it no easier.

Lumpkin's laboured breaths
became a rattle.
Cinderella stroked his head,
smiling as his ears twitched
the way they used to when
she'd rattle his food bucket.

He gazed at her one last time
with those liquid eyes
and
 his
  breathing
   stopped.

Cinderella did not cry,
she had prepared for this.
Everything would change now.
Lumpkin had been her one escape.
Her so-called family
never ventured into the fields,
never went close to Lumpkin
who never failed to bite.

Cinderella would miss his company
and his protection
now she was alone.

She picked up a spade
and began to dig.
And then it hit her,
what those carriages
reminded her of.
They looked
like ...

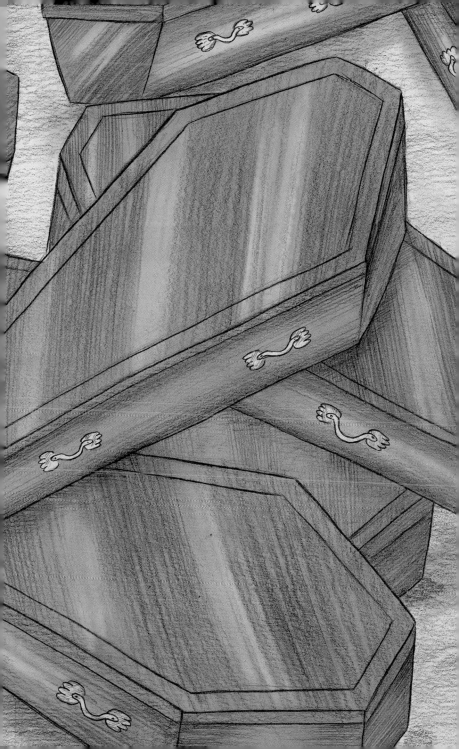

CHAPTER 2

The Prince Prepares for the Ball

It was in the cold,
dark bite of night
that the prince arrived
at the mansion.

The mansion that protruded
from the crown of Grimmsville's
only hill
like a growth –
next to the old abandoned cemetery.

Inside, the prince
was preparing
for the first
of his three balls...

"Another trio of dreary balls."

He was new in town,
was new in every town he visited.
He never stayed long.
Just long enough to host three balls
to meet the locals...

"The dull, dreary yokels."

To get the scent of the girls...

"The most beautiful girls."

He would woo one tonight...

"Savour the scent of the others
and seek them out in the nights to come."

He was bored of the balls
and the parties
and the locals
and the constant feeding.
The prince
needed a change.

His servants always made the mansion look grand. There was always a mansion on a hill in these towns.

A place too big, too old and too …

HAUNTED

for any of the locals to go near.

So, the prince would buy the mansion in advance, and send his servants ahead of his coffin-shaped carriages to carry out his orders:

"Blacken the windows!"

"Remove the garlic from the kitchen!"

"Unsharpen the pencils!"

"Cover the mirrors!"

He was a particular prince
with particular needs.

CHAPTER 3

The Three Fake Sisters

On the night of the first ball,
a fat, yellow moon lay bloated in a satin sky
and Cinderella's three beautiful sisters
were making her life

HELL!

They were not her real sisters,
not even lovely half- or step-sisters,
they were FAKE sisters.

Three beautiful FAKE sisters,
daughters of her beautiful, FAKE mother.
Not a lovely step-mother,
just a FAKE mother,
all smiles and grins in public
but behind closed doors
she was all horns, fangs and hooves.
Cinderella's FAKE mother
had killed her father!
Through nagging, cruelty
and many suspect ...

POISON!!!

Cinderella knew death,
had known it from an early age
from the early demise of her every pet:

Fluffy the dog ... squashed flat by a large rat.

Simpson the cat ... ran into an axe (twice!)

Karate the goldfish found ... drowned!!!

Drowned???

Drowned!!!

And of course,
Lumpkin the horse.

Cinderella knew death
from the long-lasting
splutter-spewing,
demise of her mother,
her real mother,
her bi-o-logical mother,
her cremated mother,
whose cinders
now sat in a skull-shaped locket
that hung from Cinderella's neck
(hence the name her FAKE mother
had pushed upon her).

"If you insist on wearing cinders around
your neck,
you shall be Cinders by name … Cinderella."

Cinderella knew death
from her own continuous bouts
of Whimsey and Achey-limb.
Cinderella knew death
and had been hardened by it.

Cinderella earned her keep:
scrubbing the black from the floors,
the scum from the baths,
the wax from the ears.
Collecting the strands of her fake sisters' hair
that collated in their pearl combs,
combs that adorned their vast dressing tables.

Dressing tables inlaid with silver
    and dotted with pearls,

ruby-encrusted
and misted with flowery smells.

All bought with Cinderella's inheritance.
Cinderella's money!
Left for her by her mother,
her real mother,
her bi-o-logical mother.

On this night, the night of the first ball,
a choked moon hung in a purple sky,
and Cinderella's three FAKE sisters were
being particularly mean.

They knew that their mother,
their beautiful mother,
their beautiful mother with a face like enamel,
like marble,
like glass:
Cold, hard but stunning...

They knew that their mother
would never let Cinderella leave
whilst the house was in a mess!

If the black was not gone from the floors,
the grime from the bath,
the wax from the ears,
Cinderella would be made to stay home,
to wear her fingers to stubs,
bloody stubs, from all the scrubbing.

"Why don't you pick out a nice dress to wear,
Cinderella?"
flapped Hebina,
the tallest of the wafer-waisted sisters,
with large, beautiful ears that tinkled in the wind.

Hebina knew full well that Cinderella
had just one dress to wear,
a dress that she would scrub every evening
and wear damp every morning.

"Why don't you get yourself a nice necklace,
something better than those cinders,
Cinderella?"
droned Storm,
the most aromatic of the wafer-waisted sisters,
who had hair that dangled past a bottom
that had never been wiped!

Storm knew full well that Cinderella would

never remove her mothers ashes from
around her neck.
*"Why don't you pick out some lovely shoes
to wear, Cinderella?"*
phlegmed Alhora,
the meanest of the wafer-waisted sisters,
who had an unusually long tongue.

She knew full well that Cinderella did not
own nice shoes!

     The girl barely owned socks!

Cinderella owned calluses!
   Hard skin carbuncles.
      The skin on her heels was so thick
        and so cracked,
that woodlice
had been known to lay eggs in them!

The cracks on her heels were so wide,
that she could open bottles with them!

The cracks on her heels were so deep
that her footsteps echoed!
        Echoed!
           Echoed!!!

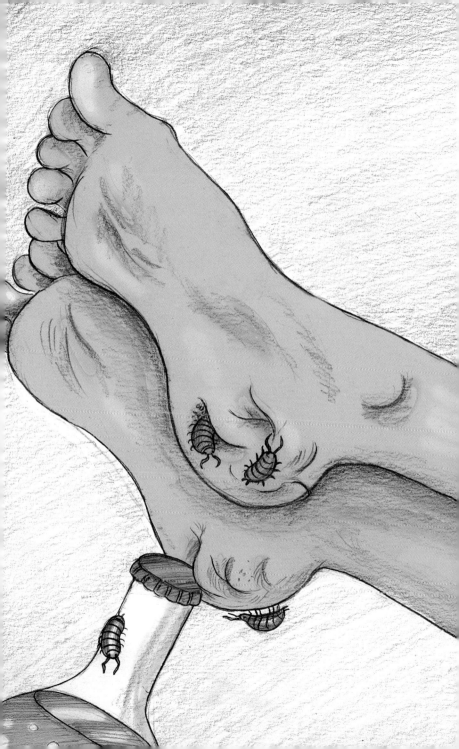

Cinderella's three FAKE, beautiful sisters
did not want Cinderella to go to the ball.
They wanted the prince all to themselves!
So they squirted toothpaste around the taps
and the sink,
     poured rubbish onto the beds,
          mixed the salt with the sugar,
               blew their noses on the curtains.

And left a slimy, slippery gift at the top of the stairs!

For they were beautiful, FAKE and foul.

Cinderella would not be going to the ball. She had:

Taps to scrub.

Rubbish to clear from beds.

Salt to de-sweeten.

Curtains to un-snot.

Her three FAKE, beautiful sisters
smiled sweetly as they sauntered out of the house.

"See you!"

snapped Hebina.

"Laters!"

droned Storm.

"You missed a bit!"

sludged Alhora.

"Cinderella, darling, do make sure the house
is spotless before we return – or there will
be hell to pay!"

breathed her ceramic, FAKE mother as
she glazed out of the door.

Cinderella,
tears jewelling in her eyes,
sighed.

She wanted to go to the ball,
not to meet a prince
but rather to get out into the world,
to breathe in the night air,
to see something other
than the dark walls of their severe abode
with its square rooms
and windows
with wire embedded into the glass.
She wanted to go to the ball to help her forget

the loss of Lumpkin.
She never saw the slimy surprise
left for her at the top of the stairs
by her three FAKE sisters.
A warm, slippery, stinking, surprise.
Cinderella squelched one foot into it ...

and she slipped!

CHAPTER 4

Cinderella and Death

Cinderella had slipped,
rolled,
tumbled
and crashed
down the winding stairs
of their pokey home!
And when she got
to the bottom,
she had ...
died!

She didn't know she was dead,
not at first,
not until she got a visit
from The Fairy of Death...

The lights of the house started to flicker...

A sick wind blew through the building

though no windows were open!

Cinderella lay on the floor,

broken,

dimly aware of a shadow
    deepening,
        darkening around her.
            The shadow of ...

"Cinderella, you have died,
It is sad but true,
You fell and hit your head,
After slipping on some poo!

Now your breath has gone,
And your heart no longer beats,
But your life has been so grim,
That I'm offering you a treat.

For three nights hence,
I shall blow life into thee,
You shall go to each ball,
You shall join the parties!

But as the clock strikes twelve,
On each night to come,
My power starts to fade,
And your life will be undone.

So rise, my dear, tonight,
Go, dance with a fella.
Make the most of my boon,
Go forth as Zombierella."

Death raised her arms.
Lightning sprang from her palms.
Cinderella jolted and shook and arose,
her face gaunt but beautiful,
her skin a peculiar shade
of moss-meets-gravestone,
of bone-meets-rot!
Her eyes dark,
her nails long.
She was a zombie.
She was ...

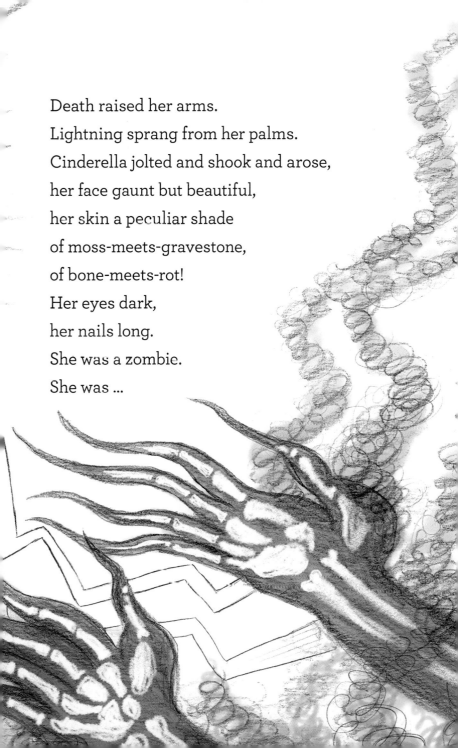

Zombierella!!!

Zombierella stood
cracking her bones back into place.
Her skin felt smooth and cold like ice.
She placed a hand to her chest
and realized...

"My heart has stopped,
But I'm not shocked.

No blood in my veins,
But I feel quite sane.

No breath from my lips,
But I'm not frighted.
I am intrigued,
I am excited!"

Death led her out to the garden,
gave her a spade
made from an arm bone and a shoulder blade,
and told her with star-twinkling eyes to...

"Dig!"

Death pointed at a grave,
the grave of Lumpkin,
Zombierella's beloved horse.

The horse she would ride
when her father had been alive,
the horse that had died
of oldness.
The horse she had buried several times
over the last three days
because her evil, FAKE mother
kept digging up the bones...

"To sell to the handsome glue-maker in town!"

Zombierella dug.
She found she was strong,
much stronger than before,
and fast.
She dug up Lumpkin in no time.
He was just a dry sack of skin covering
dusty bones.

Death clacked her fingers and Lumpkin
    twitched
        and twisted
           and shook off his dry skin
               until just his skeleton
                  remained.

Lumpkin stood,
red eyes glowing
in a bleached white skull.
He neighed
as he gazed
at Zombierella.
She nuzzled her old friend.

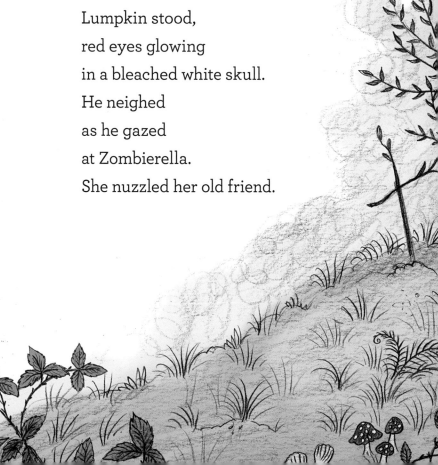

"You galloped far where I could not follow,
Left me drowning in heart-stopping sorrow,
As I faced this cruel world alone.

Now you are back with bones picked white,
My death stallion, my rattling knight,
You are my death-blessed throne."

Next Death pointed at a mushroom,
a huge, rat-grey mushroom
growing from the stump of a long-dead tree.
Death clacked the bones of her fingers
and the mushroom swelled and bloated
into the form of a coach,
    a carriage,
        a Tally-ho.
Smaller mushrooms sprouted around it,
their caps becoming wheels.
Death harnessed the bronco
to the Tally-ho.

"This will get you to the ball,"

Death chuckled.

"But you'll need some drivers!"

Death clacked her fingers
and from the graves
of Fluffy the dog
and Simpson the cat
arose two ghosts!
One flattened,
one sliced.

They woofed and purred at Zombierella
as they wafted by and took up the reigns
of Lumpkin
the skeletal horse.

Then, with a final waggle of all her bones,
Death rattled...

And the dead leaves of autumn

lifted up from the ground

and spun in the air.

They were joined by the wings

of sycamore seeds

and the husks of beech kernels.

They twisted and spun and attacked!

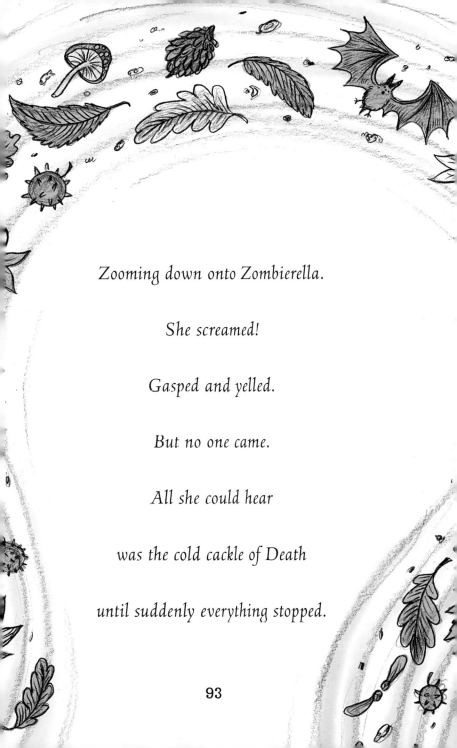

Zooming down onto Zombierella.

She screamed!

Gasped and yelled.

But no one came.

All she could hear

was the cold cackle of Death

until suddenly everything stopped.

93

Zombierella was fine.

She looked down and saw that she was dressed
in all the warm colours of autumn:
The auburns that had swum in her
mother's eyes,
the chestnut of her mother's hair,
the brown of her mother's smile.

Zombierella was off
in her mushroom carriage
with her perished pets,
bouncing over hills,
creaking over bridges,
winding her way up
to the mansion
on the top of the hill.

CHAPTER 5

The Ball

The ball was in full swing!
Dancehall music was pulsing
low and melodic,
bitter and smooth,
from the great hall.
Guests laughed, danced and nibbled
at the entrées:

Lychees stuffed with blueberries –
    to Zombierella they looked like bleeding eyes.
Doughnuts shaped like cockroaches –
    Zombierella could have sworn one of them moved.
Huge, hard-boiled eggs carved to look like faces –
    but what beast could lay such
    wondrously huge eggs?

Yet, despite all the frivolity,
Zombierella could feel a sadness
coming from the place,
a sadness as thick
as blood!

She entered the great hall
and everyone fell silent.

Zombierella looked spectacular,
frozen in time,
beautiful beyond words
in her dress of autumn leaves
and her eyes dark and deep.
No one seemed to notice her bare feet
and, if they did,
it only added to her loveliness
as her toes peeped out from the hem of her dress.
(If they had seen her heels – her dried cracked
heels – it would have been another story!)

The prince floated to her,
wrapped in black
and handsome as the night.
He took Zombierella by the hand
and they danced...

Danced like the room was empty,
danced like starlight carried their steps,
danced like neither of them had
danced before.
And while they danced,
the prince felt whole
and complete.
He totally forgot why he was here
in another mansion
in another town –
forgot his need to feed!

And Zombierella found in his grasp
something entirely new:
acceptance
and love.

The prince's red-brown eyes
saw her
in all her cold beauty.
His wolfish smile
sent electricity
over her skin.

They danced until Zombierella
spied one of her sisters slithering in the crowd
and decided to take revenge!

Zombierella's beautiful, FAKE sister Hebina ...
horrid, hateful,
Hebina
did not recognize Zombierella
as her very own fake sister.
And so Zombierella asked,
in her sweetest voice...

"Won't you join me
in the loo?"
(The way girls do!)

And Hebina,

being in awe of this beauty

who had danced with the prince all night, said...

"If I must!"

Once they were alone
Zombierella turned on her sister
and said...

"You called me stupid,
You called me names.
But if I am so stupid,
Then how come I have brains?"

Zombierella opened her mouth wide,
stuck her hand inside,
and pulled out her...

And Hebina
fainted.

Just as the clock began to...

Dong!

Zombierella had to get back.

Dong!

Death said that the magic would fade
at midnight.

Dong!

Zombierella ran from the bathroom.

Dong!

Into the great hall.

Dong!

Past the prince who called for her.

Dong!

But there was no time.

Dong!

She leapt into her mushroom carriage.

Dong!

Her ghostly pets whipped the reigns.

Dong!

Skeleton Lumpkin neighed.

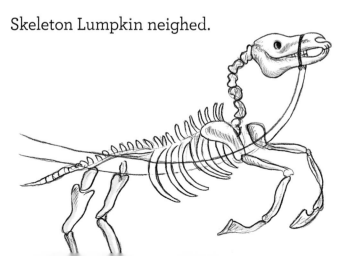

Dong!

And together they wound away from the mansion.

Dong!

Over the hills and home in time for the last...

DONG!!!

Lumpkin's bones sank down into the ground.

The pets returned to their graves.

The carriage withered back into a mushroom.

Zombierella returned to the bottom of the stairs
and died!

Yet, even though she was dead,

still she dreamed ...

and all her dreams

were of the prince and their dance.

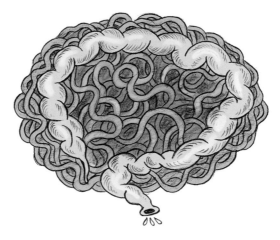

CHAPTER 6

Guts!

Hebina, Storm and Alhora
and the fake mother
stayed the night at the mansion
with the other guests.

The following morning
Hebina tried telling her sisters
what she had seen...

"Don't be mad,"
nasalized Storm.

"You're crazy,"
phlegmed Alhora.

"Rest my beauties,"
crazed their mother.

"Save your energies for the second dance.
You must not give the girl in the
leaf dress a chance."

They never would have guessed
that the girl of harvest
could be their very own Cinderella.
They thought Cinderella was at home...

Scrubbing the taps.
Clearing the beds.
De-salinating the sugar.
De-bogeying the draperies.

The sisters stayed with their mother at
the mansion all day
hoping to see the prince.

That night back at the house
Death visited Zombierella again.
With her clacking fingers,
she repeated her spell...

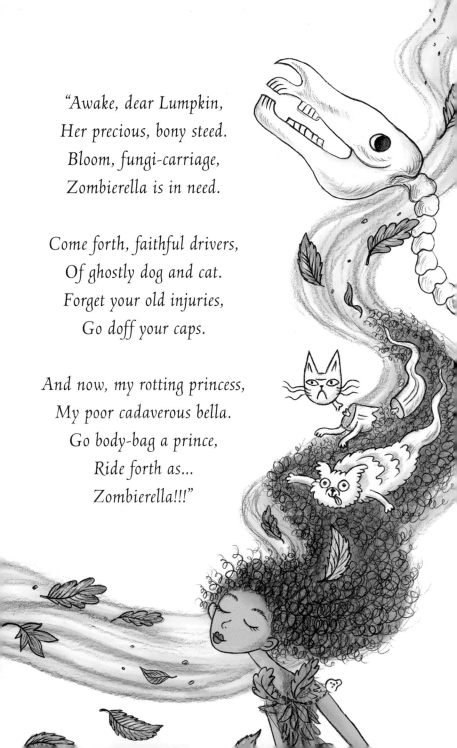

"Awake, dear Lumpkin,
Her precious, bony steed.
Bloom, fungi-carriage,
Zombierella is in need.

Come forth, faithful drivers,
Of ghostly dog and cat.
Forget your old injuries,
    Go doff your caps.

And now, my rotting princess,
My poor cadaverous bella.
Go body-bag a prince,
    Ride forth as...
    Zombierella!!!"

The prince had spent the entire day
trying to sleep.

Away from the sunlight...

"The harsh, heat-filled sunlight."

He had not slept,
he had not fed, instead
he had recalled the memory
of his dance with the girl of leaves...

"A girl unlike the others,
A girl who glides,
A girl with skin as cold as mine,
A girl who is ... inedible!"

As soon as night fell
he waited for Zombierella
in the shadows of the ball.

But in swished Storm.
Hair-swishy Storm
was desperate to dance with the prince.
But he had turned up his nose
at her every offer to...

"Boogie?"

So, Storm took it upon herself
to drag the prince on to the dance floor!

She threw him left,

she threw him right,

up
and
down!

She twirled the prince round and round.

And just when he could take no more,
when anger was making his mouth drool
and his hands claw,

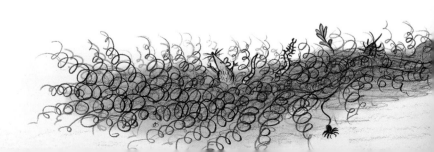

Zombierella cascaded into the great hall
even more beautiful than the night before.
Her eyes even darker.
She twirled to Storm,
took her by the arm
and whirled her out to the balcony
where they were alone...

"You called me yellow belly,
You would jibe and strut.
But if I'm such a coward,
How come I've got GUTS?"

Zombierella plunged her hand
into her belly button
and pulled out her...

Guts!!!

And Storm
fainted.

Zombierella was back in the ball,
her guts back in place,
silencing the crowd
as she danced with the prince.

His arms like a frozen bear hug
making Zombierella feel like
she belonged forever in his grasp.
And as he hugged her,
he forgot his need to feed,
    forgot his hunger,
     forgot that he was in fact a...

Vampire!!!

He had always been a vampire
for as long as he could remember.
Had always travelled with his servants
from town to town,
hosting balls for three nights
charming the locals with food and drink,
so that no one would notice the missing
until it was too late.

By the third night the prince would choose
a girl from the town to marry.
And in a parade of joy and laughter,
the locals would send him and his bride
on their way
only to realize,
when the smiles had rotted from their faces,
that a girl was missing
for every night of the ball
and no one could explain it
and no one knew why.

By the time the prince arrived at the next village,
his chosen bride
would have died!

"A blood-drained snack
for the journey."

It was the only life he'd ever known
and had he ever been gifted a choice,
he would have chosen a different life to lead.

The prince was supposed to be choosing
a mate to snack on in this Grimmsville,
but Zombierella had flowed in
and the prince had been
bewitched ... zombified!

They danced
in each other's arms
right up until the bells started to DONG...

When Zombierella once again fled home
and died
at the bottom of the stairs.
The prince felt dismay,
"Dull, dreary, dismay!"

He wanted to follow her.
He wanted to transform into a bat
and swoop down on her,
but it had been another night
that he had not fed.
His powers were weak,
he was distressed...

"I'm obsessed with the girl
in the dead leaf dress."

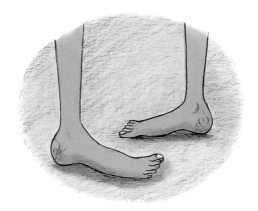

CHAPTER 7

Feet

The following morning,
still at the mansion,
Storm tried telling her sisters what she had seen.
Only Hebina believed her
and the two cried together.

"Mend yourselves together!"

chinked their mother.

"There is just one more night before the prince chooses his bride and it better be one of you."

Alhora,
angry, audaciously-tongued
Alhora
was a shoe lover.
And so,
had noticed that the girl of leaves
never wore any shoes.
And so,
she conceived a cunning plan.

Since the girl was always late...

"I'll wait
for all the stupid guests
to enter the great hall.
I'll then pour glue,
hot, thick, sticky glue
(bought from the scrumptious
glue-maker in town!)
on the steps leading up to

the big stupid dance hall.
That way
the stupid girl will get stuck outside,
leaving me free
to canoodle with the prince within."

Alhora coughed her sticky laugh
as she put her plan into place.

That night,
the third night,
Death appeared for the third and final time,
flashing her crooked teeth
and clacking her cracked fingers.

"Tonight's your final night of life,

So fill this night with beauty.

Forgive and forget all past strife,

Tonight make love your duty.

In life, many things will befall you,

Bad times and even termination!

But new life buds when love is held,

With grave-deep determination."

Death's form folded in on itself,
first shrinking, then cracking,
moulding and mildewing,
decaying until it was gone.

It being her last night on earth,
Zombierella decided to take the scenic route
to the mansion on the hill...

Past the lake where she had swum
with her mother when young,

past the orchard
where she had picked apples with her father,

past the mountain pass
where stars had screamed starlight
in her and Lumpkin's eyes.

And so she arrived at the mansion
via the back door!
And so Alhora
was in utter snotty-shock
when once again
Zombierella
glissaded into the great hall
and straight into the prince's arms.

And they danced
and danced!
Zombierella forgot her need for revenge.

"You move like frosted breath on air,
Your eyes betray a fanged nightmare,
It seems we both know hell.

Your love for me feels deep and true,
I'll savour this death-dear night with you,
If you'll only forgive my graveyard smell!"

The prince gazed into Zombierells's eyes
and forgot that this was the third night
that he had not fed,
forgot that he could no longer transform
into a bat.
And as the night drew on,
he found himself craving the comfort of a bed
instead of a coffin.

They spun as they danced,
faster and faster,
the prince giddy with Zombierella's
sweet Eau de graveyard aroma,
the room becoming a blur,
until all they could see
in the spinning
was each other.

And all was silent.
Not a breath from their mouths,
no beats in their chests,
and both realized...

"You're undead! Like me!"

The clock began to chime...
Zombierella tore herself from the prince
for the last time.
Tears tinkling in her eyes,
she ran out of the great hall,
down the steps
and stopped.
She was stuck!
Her right foot was stuck to the step,
glued to the step.
She was stuck!
Stuck to the step!
To the step she was stuck!!!
And the clock was striking!!!

She would return to lifelessness here
on the steps
for all to see.
Her prince would see her broken and dead.
(Properly dead.)
The thought filled her with dread.
So, she yanked and pulled ...

and twisted ...

her dead foot ...

off!

And left it stuck to the step.
She hopped to her waiting carriage
to be sped home
to her final resting place
at the bottom of the stairs.

The prince was left on the mansion steps
with just the foot that she had left behind.

He pulled at the foot thinking...

"This should be a shoe!"

Slid his nails underneath
and freed it from the glue.

"Whichever maiden is missing a foot
I shall make my wife,"

proclaimed the prince to all who could hear,

whilst caressing Zombierella's foot,

cracked heels and all.

Zombierella's
evil, FAKE mother
had seen the whole thing.
And being a bit sharper than her daughters,
recognized Zombierella
as her own fake daughter.

She gathered her daughters
and rushed them home
just in time ...

to watch astounded as
Zombierella's carriage withered to a mushroom.

To stare in awe as
her ghostly pets spirited back to their graves.

To gaze gobsmacked as
Zombierella staggered to the bottom of the stairs
and died
for the last time.

The mother wasted no time.
She instructed her daughters to...

"Bury her
deep in the garden,
and wipe the mess from the stairs
from where she slipped in the poo."

Bugles sounded!
The prince was swooping into town,
Zombierella's foot held aloft...

*"Whomever is missing a foot
I shall make my wife!"*

The evil, FAKE mother dragged Hebina
into the garden,
took an axe from the wood pile
and
chopped
her
foot
off!

Just as the prince arrived at their back gate.

"Woo hoo, Prince! My daughter is the princess
you seek,"

chipped the mother.

The prince approached,
Zombierella's foot in hand.
Hebina sat smiling
through tears and beads of sweat,
her foot ... adrift!

"This cannot be my princess," said the prince.
"Unless my princess has two right feet!"

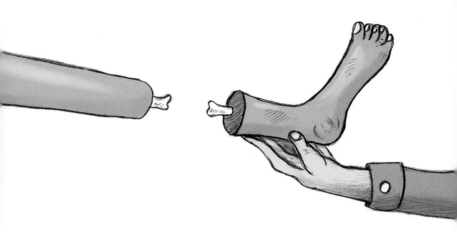

In her haste the mother had cut off
the wrong foot...
The left foot!!!

Storm had noticed the error
and whilst Hebina
pleaded for the prince to take her,
Storm went to the garden shed,
got hold of a saw

and

sawed

her

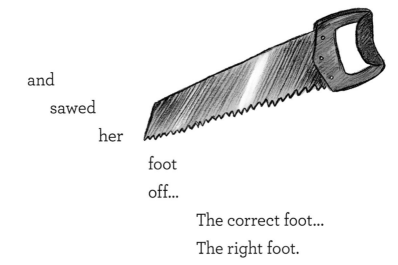

foot

off...

The correct foot...
The right foot.

And presented herself to the prince.

"My lord ... I am your princess," drooled Storm.

The prince took Zombierella's foot and held it to
Storm's stump.
But in her haste,
the girl had cut off not just the foot,
but also a considerable part of her leg.

"You cannot be my princess," said the prince.
*"Unless my princess had one leg shorter than
the other."*

Alhora was cunning.
She watched her sisters' failures diligently,
and whilst they cried and weeped
without their feet,
Alhora took a pair of scissors from the kitchen
and, with her tongue thoughtfully
up one nostril,

she carefully snipped off the correct foot,
the right foot
just above the ankle,
and presented herself to the prince.
This time the prince could not be sure...
The correct foot,
the right foot,
was missing!
And when placed under Alhora's stump,
it seemed to match.

But as he inspected her remaining foot,
Alhora's real foot,
the prince noticed the smooth baby-soft skin
of her sole and heel...
He compared it to the hard,
cracked, dry skin of Zombierella's foot,
a foot that had seen hard work
and labour

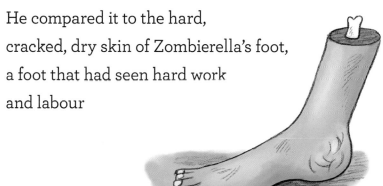

and life.

"You are not my princess," said the prince.
*"Unless my princess has never worked a day
in her life."*

That's when the prince noticed
the state of the stairs.
The sisters,
having never cleaned before in their lives,
were terrible at it.
There was dirt,
brown and dried
on the steps
where Zombierella had slipped in poo.
And in the dirt the prince could see
drag marks.
He followed the drag marks to the garden,
noticed the freshly dug soil
and with a cry of anguish ordered the sisters to ...

They hopped,
cried
and dug
like mewling pirates
terrified of the treasure below
until they uncovered
Zombierella.
A dead Zombierella.

The prince placed her foot
against the stump of her leg.

They were a perfect match.
He held her corpse to him
and for the first time
ever
he cried.
Vampires never cry,
because to cry takes big emotions
and vampires tend to be hollow,
but this vampire,
this prince, who had not fed
in three days,

who could no longer transform into a bat,
who found himself craving the comfort of a bed
instead
of a coffin,
cried for the bride he had lost.
He pressed his mouth against hers
and delivered a kiss,
not a kiss of fangs and bite,
but a proper kiss.
A kiss of love, warmth and life.

As he kissed his corpse bride
he could feel his flesh start to warm,
he could feel his teeth start to straighten
and in his chest,
he could feel his heart begin to beat.

His beating heart was joined by another,
a beat matching his own
in the chest of Zombierella
as warmth flooded her flesh,
as blood swam through her veins,
as she started to live.

Zombierella arose
no longer a zombie,
she was alive and warm and beautiful.
And as she gazed at her vampire prince,
she saw that he had changed.
He was no longer a vampire,
he was warm
and alive and beautiful.

"Dear old Death said love has power,
And now you are alive like me.
Our lives are entwined like blooming flowers,
We can live together happily."

The townsfolk gathered around
and cheered and wept
but Cinderella's evil, FAKE sisters
and horrible, FAKE mother
were nowhere to be seen.

A bang, a crash and a clatter
were heard from within.
The crowd went into the house
and there at the bottom of the stairs
were Hebina, Storm, Alhora and their mother
covered in filth, bruised and tangled.

The mother had worked out that
Cinderella's transformation
had come on account of her slipping
in poo and falling down the stairs
and so had attempted to repeat her glory.
The mother had instructed her daughters
to smear themselves
in the yucky, icky, sticky stuff
and to fling themselves,
bleeding stumps and all,
    down
       the
          steps!

But they did not die.

Death did not visit them.

They were not turned into princesses.

Cinderella and her living prince
made a home in the mansion
on the top of the hill.
The prince no longer hungered for blood,
no longer had to trek from town to town
and they settled down
in the mansion
on the top
of the hill.

They re-opened the cemetery,
cleared the weeds from the graves,
grew flowers for the dead
and gave their love and support
to all those who needed it.

And, over time,
they even had space
for Cinderella's step-mother

(who was no longer fake)
and three step-sisters
(who were no longer foul)
And over the years
they all learned to live together
as equals.

CHAPTER 8

A Shifting of Bones

Months had fruited
since Cinderella and her prince's
new living life
had begun.

The first thing they had done
on moving to the mansion
was to move the graves of her father
and her beloved pets
to the cemetery
that nestled up
to the mansion's side.

Their home was always busy,
full of love and laughter,
occasionally sadness and tears,
as they took on the role
of funeral directors
whenever a death occurred in the town.
But for the most part,
they grew flowers in their cemetery.
People came from miles around
to purchase the cut stems
and watch the sisters
who happily toiled
in the cemetery
sowing seeds
and tending the flowers:
Blood-red roses,
and skull-white tulips,
bruised dahlias
and bile-yellow lilies.

Their displays
were sought
for funerals, births
and weddings alike.
Their scents always
comforted.
Their sight
always pleased.

It was on one
of those heady spring evenings
when the sun was low,
showing its heart,
that Cinderella found herself
clearing the weeds
from Lumpkin's grave.
With one hand
holding her skull-shaped pendant
brimming with her mother's cinders,
she hummed a
low, melodic tune
of joy and sadness,
of contentment
and longing.

When, to her surprise,
the earth beneath the weeds
started to shift,
the ground started to rise,
and bone
by bleached white bone
her beloved Lumpkin
assembled.

His ruby eyes were
full of adoration
for his Cinderella.
His dried bones
full of new,
uncanny life.

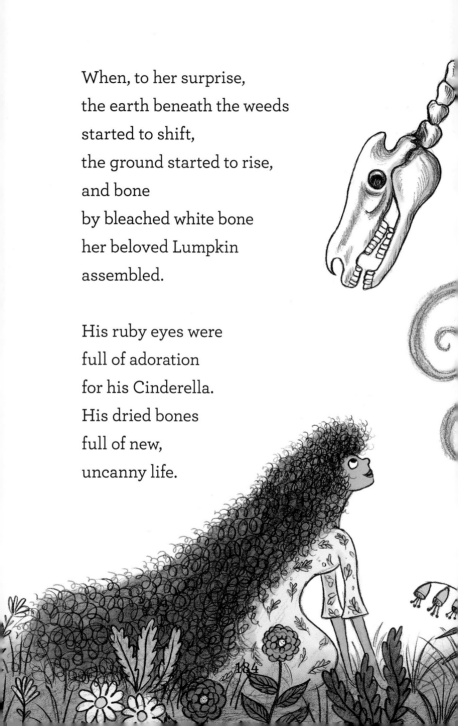

Cinderella mounted
her ossified steed
and they galloped
and clanked,
trotted and clattered
through the cemetery
past her waving sisters:

    Hebina smiling sweetly,
    great earrings in each great ear.
    Storm with hair tied back,
    a sweet carnation in her plaits.
    Alhora singing
    in her thick, strong voice.

They galloped
past the mansion
and her step-mother
who sat sipping tea
from a mismatched-chipped set.
Past her love, her prince,
who waved and laughed
his throaty guffaw
through blinding teeth
from the shade of the mansion stoop,
where he carefully applied sun lotion.
(Old habits die hard).

187

Cinderella and Lumpkin galloped
past the orchard
where apple blossom bloomed.
Past the lake
where mayflies swooned.
Past the mountain pass
where her laughter
shot up to the sky.

And from atop the mountain
where the snow caps gleamed,
she swore she could hear
the cold, loving cackle of Death
echoing around her,
echoing through her,
making Cinderella's teeth chatter
and her fingers clack!

EPILOGUE

I hope you enjoyed
that rotten tale of Zombierella.
I better put this book away
before I get a nasty bite.

I must leave you now.
I can hear books rattling their chains,
creaking their spines
and shredding their pages.
I better go and organize
the forgotten bookshelf
where this and many more
nasty tales are lurking.
I better dust off their covers
and check no books have escaped.

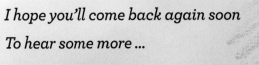

I hope you'll come back again soon
To hear some more ...

Fairy Tales Gone Bad!